THREE WAYS TO BE BRAVE

a trio of stories

words by
Karla Clark

art by
Jeff Östberg

RISE
NEW YORK

To Connor Eck, agent and friend, and John Sentovich, brother-in-law
and champion—you both have taught me more than three ways to be brave
—KC

To my family, my amazing friends, and my love Genevieve
for always supporting and inspiring me
—JÖ

RISE x Penguin Workshop

An Imprint of Penguin Random House LLC, New York

Text copyright © 2021 by Karla Clark. Illustrations copyright © 2021 by Jeff Östberg. All rights reserved. Published by Rise × Penguin Workshop, an imprint of Penguin Random House LLC, New York. The W colophon is a registered trademark and the RISE colophon is a trademark of Penguin Random House LLC. Manufactured in China.

Visit us online at www.penguinrandomhouse.com.

The text is set in P22 Platten Neu Pro.
The art was created in Photoshop.

Edited by Cecily Kaiser
Designed by Maria Elias

Library of Congress Cataloging-in-Publication Data is available upon request.

ISBN 9780593222423   10 9 8 7 6 5 4 3 2 1

TABLE of CONTENTS

Under Covers

A THUNDERSTORM

Moon's out,
Quiet house.

Cozy bed,
Clouds overhead.

Night-light,
Tucked in tight.

Rain starts,
Dog barks.

Thunder! Boom!
Shakes the room!

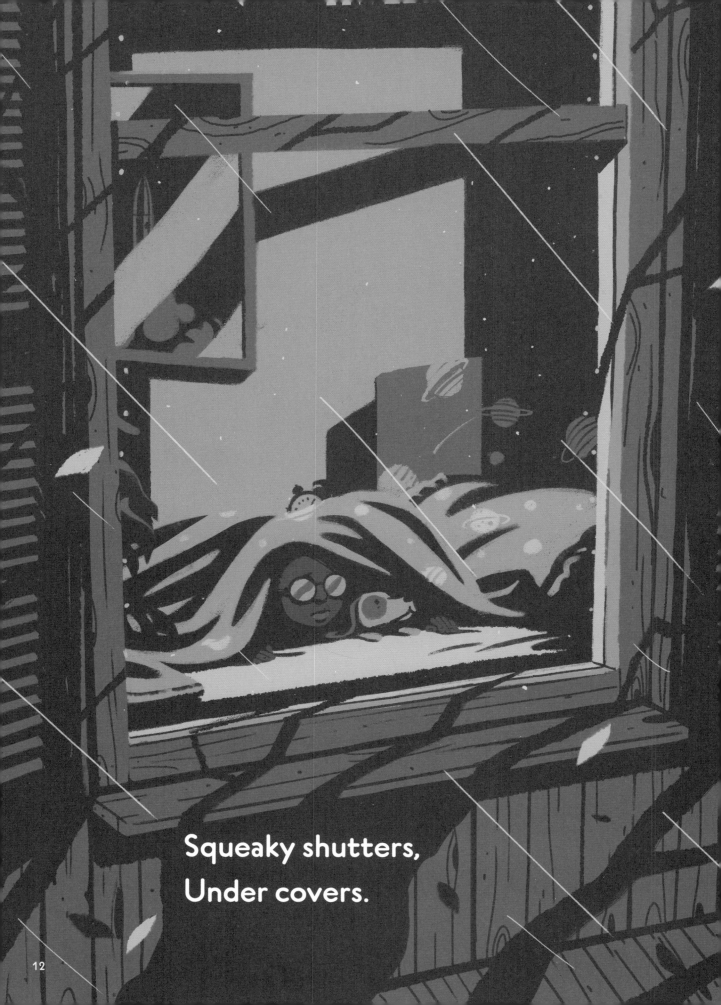

Squeaky shutters,
Under covers.

Winds pound,
Jump down.

Tiptoe,
Shadow.

Lightning flash!
Time to dash!

Run, zoom
Toward parents' room.

Hear a call
Down the hall.

Tearful sob,
Turn the knob.

Baby sis,
Hug and kiss.

Thunder roars.
Baby snores.

Flash of lightning,
Not so frightening.

Thunder blast.
Safe at last.

Nervous Belly

THE FIRST DAY OF SCHOOL

Sunrise,
Wide eyes.

Nervous belly,
Toast with jelly.

Backpack,
Lunch sack.

First-day woes,
Kiss on nose.

Daddy takes me.
Stomach aches me.

School looms tall.
Feeling small.

Girls and boys,
Lots of noise.

Tug on sleeve:
Please don't leave!

Teachers greet,
Take our seats.

Daddy goes,
Doors close.

Tear in eye,
Just might cry!

Next to me,
A girl named Bree.

She looks glum,
Sucks her thumb.

Time for art:
Decorate hearts.

One for me
And one for Bree!

Play a bunch,

Then eat lunch.

Skip and run,
Having fun!

Swing so high,
Kick the sky.

Cozy nook,
Share a book.

Clean up supplies,
Say our goodbyes.

Daddy waves.
Glad I stayed.

First day ends
With a brand-new friend.

Got the Jitters

CHECKUP DAY

Car ride,
Mommy drives.

On our way,
Checkup day.

Got the jitters,
Hug my critters.

Parking lot.
Please no shot!

Sixth floor,
Open door.

Wait and wait,
Doctor is late.

Watch the fish
Swim and swish.

Nerves are jumpy,
Feeling grumpy.

Play a game,
Hear my name.

Weight and height.
Good eyesight.

Wait some more,
Watch the door.

Doctor arrives,
Gives high fives.

Checks eyes and ears,
A couple of tears.

Checks heart and lungs,
Stick out tongue.

Time for a shot?
I think not!

Jump to the floor.
Head for the door.

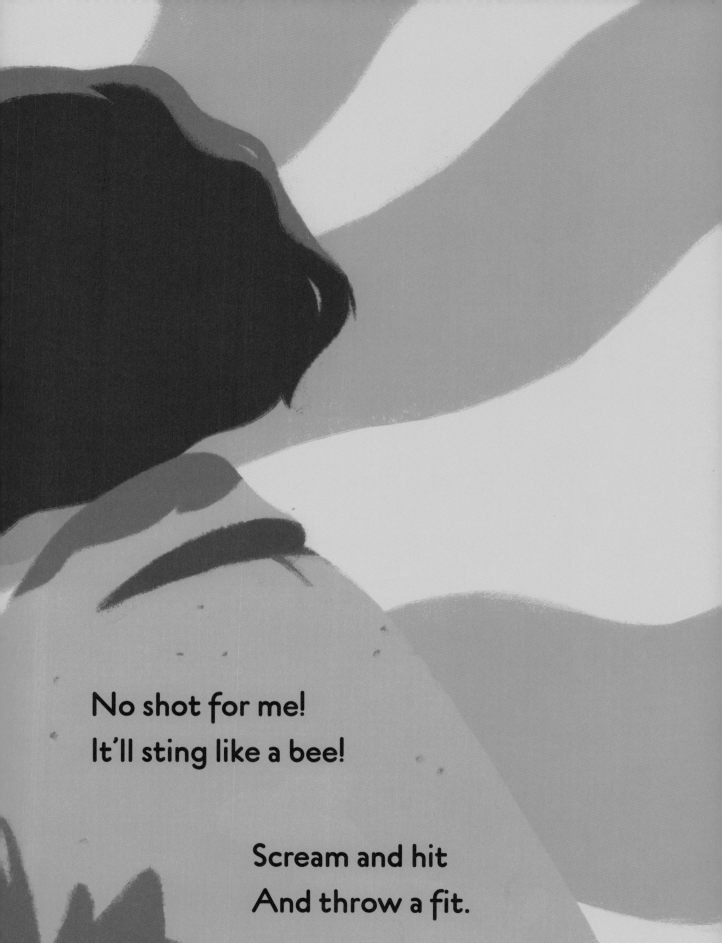

No shot for me!
It'll sting like a bee!

Scream and hit
And throw a fit.

"I understand."
Nurse takes my hand.

"Use your brain
To ease the pain!"

What do I like?
Riding my bike!

Close my eyes,
Go for a ride.

Breathe fresh air,
Wind in my hair.

One little prick . . .
It's over quick.

Pedal fast!
The pain won't last.

Open my eyes,
Blow a big sigh.

"A sticker for you
For making it through!"

Checkup complete.
Hop to my feet.

It's okay that I cried.
Being brave means I tried.